Change Is in the Air, Mallory

For my readers

And special thanks to Stacey Shoer,
for introducing me to Friendship Cake
—L.B.F.

For my mom and dad, who continue
to be amazing and supportive parents
and grandparents
—J.K.

Change Is in the Air, Mallory

by Laurie Friedman

illustrations by Jennifer Kalis

darbycreek

MINNEAPOLIS

CONTENTS

A WORD FROM MALLORY

My name is Mallory McDonald, like the restaurant but no relation. I'm ten years old. I have a brother named Max and a cat named Cheeseburger. I live on a street called Wish Pond Road, and my best friends, Mary Ann, Joey, and Chloe Jennifer, live there too.

There are lots of things my friends and I like doing together. We like eating doughnuts, hanging out at the wish pond, skateboarding, teaching new tricks to our pets, baking cookies, watching TV, painting our toenails (except for Joey), and having sleepovers (also except for Joey).

I like all these things, but there's one thing I don't like, and that's change.

I'm not talking about the nickel and dime kind that jingles in your pocket. I'm talking about the kind

6

that happens to your life and makes it totally different.

That's the kind of change that's happening to me right now.

This summer, Mary Ann and Joey will be moving to a new house that is NOT on Wish Pond Road. Now that baby Charlie is part of their family, their parents say they need a bigger house, and the house they are moving to is on the other side of Fern Falls.

And to make matters worse, Chloe Jennifer will be gone this summer too. She and her parents will be in Atlanta visiting their family and friends.

Mom says my friends will still be my friends wherever they are, and that we will find ways to see each other and to keep in touch.

She also says that change can be a good thing. But mom and I are having what she calls a "difference of opinion."

I've thought a lot about the changes that are going on in my life, and I just don't see how they will be good for me.

THE FINAL BELL

"Class, for the last time of the year, please take out your math books."

Classroom 404 at Fern Falls Elementary fills with the sounds of students who don't like that idea. My voice is one of them.

"I can't believe Mr. Knight is making us do math on the last day of school," I say to Mary Ann, who sits in the desk next to me.

Mary Ann throws her hands up in the air and grins like it doesn't bother her.

"Who cares!?!" she says. "It's the last day of school, and in exactly one hour and four minutes, summer officially begins!"

Mary Ann gives me an *I-don't-see-how-you-could-be-anything-but-happy* look.

Even though I'll be glad to be done with school, there are a couple of reasons why I'm not so happy that summer is here.

For starters, Mary Ann and Joey and the rest of the Winston family are moving across town to a bigger house. In exactly one week, they'll no longer be my next-door neighbors. I won't be able to walk next door and hang out with them whenever I want, which is most of the time. On top of that, Chloe Jennifer is leaving this weekend to go back to Atlanta.

I don't even want to think about the long, hot summer on Wish Pond Road without my best friends.

"Math books, please." Mr. Knight's voice interrupts my thoughts.

He taps his fingers on his desk like he doesn't like having to ask twice. He waits until everyone's books are opened and on their desks.

Then he smiles. "Just kidding," he says with a laugh. "It's party time!"

Everyone cheers as books slam shut and Mr. Knight pulls out party supplies. He has cups and plates and lemonade. He even brought cookies and fruit.

"Who wants a sugar cookie with sprinkles?" he asks.

"Those look delicious!" says Chloe Jennifer.

My friends all take cookies as Mr. Knight carries the platter from desk to desk.

"Mmm!" says my friend Pamela as she bites into a cookie.

"Mallory, would you like one?" asks Mr. Knight.

"No thanks," I tell my teacher. His cookies look delicious, but I'm not in a cookie mood.

Pamela frowns. "Mallory, you never say no to cookies."

She looks at me like she's a doctor and I'm her patient and she's trying to figure out what's wrong with me. "I get it," she says. "You're sad that the school year is ending." Then she leans closer like what she's about to say is for my ears only. "I'm always sad when the school year is over too."

She makes a frowny face. "It's so boring in the summer when you don't have anything you're supposed to study or read."

I nod at Pamela like she guessed what's wrong with me. Then I take a cookie. It's easier than telling Pamela what's really wrong. She's a really good student, so I get why she's upset that school is ending. But I'm upset for totally different reasons.

I take a bite of my cookie and fake-smile like I'm having a good time just like everyone else.

If I tell Pamela I'm upset because Mary Ann and Joey are moving and Chloe Jennifer will be away all summer, she'll just say we can hang out together this summer. Pamela is a good friend, and I like doing things with her. But it's not the same as hanging out with my friends on my street.

"Everyone, settle down," says Mr. Knight. Then he goes around the room asking everyone what they're doing over the summer.

"I'm going to jewelry-making camp," says Zoe.

"I'm going to stay at my aunt's farm for two weeks." Pamela tells the class that her aunt is an organic farmer and that she's going to help her with her crops.

Arielle and Danielle are taking dance lessons. Pete is playing in a basketball league. Zack is going on a trip to California.

I try to listen while everyone talks about camps and trips and lessons and leagues. But it's hard to focus on what everyone will be doing when I'm thinking about what I won't be doing.

When Mr. Knight gets to Mary Ann, she tells the class that she and Joey are moving. "Since we have a new baby brother, we need a bigger house."

"The house is cool," says Joey. "We each get our own room."

Mary Ann and Joey both sound excited as they tell the class about their new house.

"Mallory, what will you be doing?" asks Mr. Knight.

"At the end of the summer, we're taking a family trip to the Grand Canyon," I tell my class.

Everyone *oohs* and *ahs* like going to the Grand Canyon will be supercool. Mr. Knight says that the Grand Canyon is one of the wonders of the world and that I should take lots of pictures.

I smile like I'm excited. And I *am* excited about that. I'm just not excited about what's happening at the beginning of the summer.

Mr. Knight finishes going around the room. When he's done, he looks at the clock. There are only a few minutes before the bell rings one last time.

Mr. Knight straightens his pen-and-pencil tie, and then he makes a speech about what a smart group of kids we are and what a pleasure we've been to teach. "You will all make excellent fifth graders," he says.

Then he says it's time for an annual tradition in his classroom. "You can all help me do the countdown." He points to the clock, and we all count together.

Ten. Nine. Eight. Seven. Six. Five. Four. Three. Two. One.

When the final bell rings, my classmates clap and cheer and grab their backpacks. As we leave classroom 404 for the last time, I know everyone is happy because that bell means the end of school.

But for me, it means the end of a whole lot more.

UP IN SMOKE

"Raise your right hand if you want chicken and your left hand if you want a hot dog," says Frank. Joey and Max raise both hands, which means they want chicken and a hot dog. Everybody laughs. Well, almost everybody.

If you ask me, this barbecue is no laughing matter.

It's the Winstons' annual *end-of-school* barbecue. Last year it was a lot of fun.

We spent the whole afternoon eating chicken and hot dogs and playing cards and board games. But this year things are different.

Not only is it the last barbecue the Winstons will host on Wish Pond Road, but it's also a going-away party for the Jackson-Browns, who are leaving for Atlanta in the morning. If I were at the wish pond right now, I'd make a wish that all my friends weren't leaving this summer. But I know there's no hope of that wish coming true.

I guess Frank can tell that something is bothering me because he closes the lid of the grill and walks over to me. He puts his chef's hat on my head. That usually makes me laugh, but not this time. "What's wrong, Mal?" he asks in a low voice.

"Nothing," I say.

Frank adjusts the chef's hat so it covers one of my eyes. "You look very stylish," he says with a smile.

I try to smile back, but Frank isn't fooled.

He puts an arm around me. "C'mon, Mallory. You know how much I like to barbecue. We're going to have our same *end-of-school* barbecue next year. The only difference will be that it will be at our new house."

I smile at Frank even though what he said doesn't make me feel much better. All I can think about is that one week from today, my best friends will be living in their new house and there will be someone else living here.

Even though Colleen told us that the people who bought their house are nice, the only thing I know for sure is that they won't be Mary Ann and Joey.

Frank pushes the chef's hat out of my eyes like he wants to say something important. But he's not the one who says anything. Winnie is.

"There's smoke coming out of the grill!" she yells.

Frank grabs his hat off my head and runs to the grill. He pushes back the lid and starts flipping chicken and hot dogs. "Just in time," he says.

He motions for everyone to grab a plate, and he starts piling them high with chicken and hot dogs. There's salad and corn and baked beans. Everyone fills plates and sits down at the picnic table in the Winstons' backyard.

"The chicken is delicious," Mom says to Frank.

"It almost went up in smoke," he says.

My parents, Colleen, Grandpa Winston, and the Jackson-Browns all laugh at Frank's barbecue humor. Max, Joey, Winnie, Mary Ann, and Chloe Jennifer look like they thought it was funny too. Even baby Charlie is smiling like he can tell someone made a joke.

But I can't laugh. It feels like chicken and hot dogs aren't the only things going up in smoke. I can't imagine what this summer is going to be like when Mary Ann, Joey, and Chloe Jennifer are all gone. I try not to think about it and just focus on the conversation at the table. But that's not so easy to do. The Winstons are talking about their new house, and the Jackson-Browns are talking about what they're going to do this summer in Atlanta.

When dinner is over, Mom brings out a chocolate cake she baked. "It's a going-away cake," she says. As she cuts extra-big slices for everyone, Dad makes a speech. He wishes the Winstons good luck in their new home and tells the Jackson-Browns that he hopes they have safe travels tomorrow.

When everyone finishes eating the cake, Chloe Jennifer's dad looks at his watch. "We'd better head home," he says. "It's a long drive tomorrow, so we're leaving at 4 a.m."

Chloe Jennifer and her mother groan like they're not too happy about their departure time.

"I guess we'll have to say good-bye tonight," Chloe Jennifer says to Mary Ann and me. We all stand up and give each other a big hug.

I feel a lump in my throat. "I'm going to miss you," I say to Chloe Jennifer.

"Me too," Mary Ann tells her.

Chloe Jennifer smiles like she appreciates hearing that. "We can all be pen pals this summer," she says.

Chloe Jennifer's parents tell everyone good-bye. Then the Jackson-Browns leave for their house. When I get to my house, I go into my room and shut the door. Tonight was the first of what will be two good-byes. This one was a little easier because at least I know Chloe Jennifer is coming back at the end of the summer.

But in one week, Mary Ann and Joey will be gone for good.

I sit down at my desk and pull out the list I made before dinner. I was going to give it to Frank and Colleen at the barbecue and try to convince them to stay on Wish Pond Road. But I knew I couldn't.

10 REASONS why I, Mallory McDonald, Think the WINSTON Family Should NOT Move!

Reason #1: There might be rats or snakes or mice in your new house. (Or all three!)

Reason #2: Your new neighbors could be mean, rude, smelly, or LOUD!

Reason #3: If your neighbors are loud, it will wake your sleeping baby! (Remember: Babies need their sleep!) It will also wake you! (Babies aren't the only ones who need their sleep!)

Reason #4: There might be a mean dog that lives on your street. That mean dog might like to eat babies (the second baby reminder!) or parents, grandparents, and older kids too!!!

Reason #5: There might be an infectious disease on your street! Infectious diseases are VERY, VERY, VERY bad for babies! (The third and final baby reminder!)

Reason #6: There won't be a wish pond on your street. Do you really think Mary Ann and Joey will be happy if you move to a street without a wish pond?!?

Reason #7: If you move, Mary Ann and Joey won't live on a street with a best friend on it. Trust me, there is NO WAY they will be happy if you move to a street where they won't have a best friend.

Reason #8: If you move, *you* will be unhappy because you will spend lots of time driving them back to Wish Pond Road to visit me. You will have to spend a lot of money on gas. Will that make you happy?!?

Reason #9: If you move, I will be unhappy because my best friends won't live next door to me anymore. I will cry a lot, which means...

Reason #10: My parents will have to spend lots of money on tissues, so they won't be happy either!

Do you really want all these people to be unhappy? I didn't think so. There is a solution: PLEASE, PLEASE, PLEASE DON'T MOVE!!!!!!

When I finish reading my list, I crumple it up and throw it in the trash. Whether I like it or not, I know the Winstons are moving.

And there's nothing I can do to stop them.

A LATE-NIGHT TALK

"What's your problem?" asks Max.

I shake my head at him and make some *it's-hard-to-talk-with-a-mouth-full-of-toothpaste* sounds.

"Whatever," says Max like he gave me a shot and I blew it. He wipes his mouth on a towel.

I spit out my toothpaste. I'd like to tell

my brother what my problem is. If anyone should get it, it should be Max. He's got the same problem.

"I'm upset because Joey and Mary Ann are moving," I say.

Max looks at me like that doesn't count as a problem.

I can't believe I have to explain this to my brother. "You should be upset too," I say. "Winnie is moving. You're not going to live next door to your girlfriend anymore."

Max shrugs. "What's the big deal? She's not moving to China. I'll still see her."

It might not be a big deal to Max, but it's a big deal to me. I wipe my mouth and go to my room. "Whatever," I say. There's no use trying to talk to my brother about anything.

I get in bed and pull Cheeseburger next to me. I pet the fur between her ears, and then I turn out the light. But I can't fall asleep. I have to talk to somebody. I slide my feet into my fuzzy duck slippers and head upstairs.

Mom and Dad's door is open. I stick my head inside. "May I talk to you?" I ask softly.

"Mallory!" Both my parents say my name at the same time. I can tell they're surprised to see me. Dad pats the space on the bed between them.

"What's wrong?" asks Mom.

I plop down on the bed between them and take a deep breath. "In just one week, I won't have any friends on Wish Pond Road," I say.

Mom and Dad look at each other like they're trying to decide who should talk first.

Mom does. "Mallory, just because Mary Ann and Joey are moving doesn't mean you won't see them."

"I know. But it won't be the same. I won't be able to knock on Mary Ann's window whenever I want to talk to her or walk to the wish pond with Joey anytime we feel like it. And Chloe Jennifer won't be around either."

"But she'll be back at the end of the summer," Dad reminds me.

"And you're going to be pen pals," says Mom.

"I know. But that's not as much fun as actually doing things with someone." I look down and pick a fuzz ball off the blanket. "I just don't get why they all had to leave at the same time."

Dad wraps an arm around me. "Sweet Potato, you're going to be fine. Change is scary. But do you remember how scared you were when we moved to Fern Falls?"

I nod. Dad pulls me in next to him and keeps talking. "You had to leave Mary Ann behind then. But you wrote letters and visited each other." Mom picks up where Dad leaves off. "Who would have thought that Colleen and Frank would meet, fall in love, and get married and that Mary Ann would be your next-door neighbor again?"

Mom pauses, then keeps talking. "And then baby Charlie was born. That was a big change, but you've adjusted to it. Now you enjoy having Charlie around, don't you?"

I nod.

"So you never know what might happen," Mom says. "Change just means things are different, but not necessarily bad. Lots of times, change is good."

I let out a deep breath. Mom has been saying this to me a lot lately. "I get what you're saying. But still, I know it won't be easy when they're all gone."

Dad rubs my back. "It might not be, but you'll get through it. And you might even find that some unexpectedly good things happen."

Mom nods in agreement. "We're here for you," she says. "And soon, Grandma will be here for her visit. Then a few weeks after that, we leave for the Grand Canyon."

Dad smiles at me. "What do you say we make a deal?"

I can't help but smile. Dad knows I like to make deals.

"Try your best to have a good attitude about Mary Ann and Joey moving," says Dad.

I nod. "I can try to do that." Then I give Dad a *what-do-I-get-in-return* look.

Dad smiles like he was waiting for me to ask. "You do that and Mom and I will let you stay in our bed and watch a movie

with us." He extends
his hand like he wants
me to shake it if I
accept the terms.

I shake Dad's hand.
I'd really like to stay
up and watch a movie.
"Deal!" I say.

I just hope I can hold up my end of
the bargain.

SAYING GOOD-BYE

Five days ago, I made my deal with Dad that I would try to have a good attitude about Mary Ann and Joey moving.

I've tried, but it hasn't been easy. So many things have happened in these last five days that have made it hard.

In fact, just about everything that has happened these last five days has been

hard because everything that's happened
has been about their move.

I feel like it's pretty much the only thing
anyone on Wish Pond Road is talking
about. And to be honest, it has made it
very hard to have a good attitude about it.

If you don't believe me, keep reading
and you'll see what I mean.

Five Days Ago

I decided to go next door to help Mary
Ann and Joey, who were supposed to be
spending the day packing their rooms. I
remember when I moved to Fern Falls how
hard it was to pack, so I thought they'd
both be happy I was there helping them.

But it was almost like I wasn't there at all.

I helped Joey and Mary Ann put clothes
and shoes and all their other stuff in boxes.
It took us all morning.

We packed box after box of shoes, clothes, books, rain gear, and Mary Ann's jewelry and hair thingies. When we got to her scrapbooks, I said we should take a break and look at them. "We can look back at all the fun stuff we've done together on Wish Pond Road," I said.

I thought it was a really good idea.

But Mary Ann didn't agree. "Mallory, I don't have time to take a break." She said it like I'd just suggested she do something really crazy, like stick her head in the toilet.

My feelings were hurt because it seemed like she did have time to take a break. She wasn't moving for five more days. But I was trying to have a good attitude about their move, so I didn't say anything. I just kept packing.

But while I was putting her scrapbooks in a box, Joey and Winnie came in her room

and Winnie said they all needed to talk about who was getting which room in the new house.

While I was packing scrapbooks, they were talking about where they were going to sleep and who would have to share a bathroom! It was like they forgot I was even there.

I reminded Mary Ann that she said she didn't have time for a break.

But she said she wasn't taking one. "I'm discussing important moving matters," she said.

Then she, Joey, and Winnie went right on talking about their new house, and it made me feel like the one thing that didn't matter was me.

Four Days Ago

I went outside to get the mail, and I saw my neighbor Mrs. Black getting her mail. She said she was very glad she had run into me. I couldn't imagine why she was, but she told me. "Mallory, I heard that your friends are leaving Wish Pond Road."

I nodded, and then I waited for Mrs. Black to say how sad that must be, but that's not what she said.

"Mallory, I'll be planting a garden this summer. Since you won't have any friends around, I thought you might like to help me."

At first, I thought Mrs. Black was joking, but then she put her arm around me and told me she'd be my new BFF.

"I bet you didn't think an old lady would know a term like that!" she said. Then she laughed like she'd just made a really funny joke.

I laughed too, to be polite. But to be honest, I didn't see what was so funny.

Three Days Ago

I decided to see how things would be without Mary Ann and Joey, so I did a little test run. I watched *Fashion Fran*—by myself. I went to the wish pond—by myself. I skateboarded—by myself. I even had a conversation by myself about what it was like doing things without my friends.

MALLORY: So how was your day by yourself?

MALLORY: Kind of lonely.

MALLORY: I'm sorry to hear that.

MALLORY: Thanks. That makes me feel better.

But I didn't feel better for long because Max heard me talking to myself and said that the only thing that would be better than my friends leaving Wish Pond Road is if they were taking me with them.

I told Max I couldn't have agreed more.

Two Days Ago

I got a letter from Chloe Jennifer. She told me about her family's long drive to Atlanta and how her dad sang songs all the way there (and that he's a really bad singer!). She told me that when she got to her grandma's house in Atlanta, her

grandma had baked chocolate chip cookies (Chloe Jennifer's favorite!) and brownies (her other favorite!). And she told me that her old friends threw a surprise *Welcome Back!* party for her.

I decided to write her a letter back. I told her about everything that's going on in my life. I told her about helping Mary Ann and Joey pack and about crazy Mrs. Black saying she wanted to be my new BFF and about doing the things I usually do with my friends, by myself.

But when I reread my letter, I ripped it up and threw it away.

I couldn't believe that the only thing I'd written about was the Winstons' move! I was doing the same thing I was complaining that everyone else was doing, which was talking about the move.

As much as I didn't want to be talking

about that, it was like my brain wouldn't let me talk about anything else!

Yesterday

   Things weren't any better yesterday.

   Since the Winstons were moving the next day (which is now today), Mary Ann and I decided to have our last sleepover ever while we both still lived on Wish Pond Road.

   I wanted everything to be perfect, so I planned out all the details. Mary Ann and I were going to do all our favorite things: watch *Fashion Fran*, bake cookies, paint our toenails, and wear our matching cupcake pajamas.

   We watched *Fashion Fran* and baked cookies and painted our toenails, but when it was time to put on our matching pajamas, Mary Ann asked if she could borrow a T-shirt to sleep in.

"You were supposed to bring your cupcake pajamas," I said.

But Mary Ann said she couldn't because they were packed. I gave Mary Ann a T-shirt. I wasn't going to make a big deal about it, but as we were going to sleep, it was kind of bothering me, so I said, "We've always worn matching pajamas at our sleepovers."

I waited for Mary Ann to say something like, *I know. It's too bad mine were packed.* But she didn't. "Maybe it's time to do new things," she said.

Then she said I should turn out the light because she needed to get some sleep since she's moving tomorrow. So I turned out the light.

Mary Ann fell right asleep. But I couldn't fall asleep for a long time.

As I lay there in my cupcake pajamas, all I could think about were all the things that were changing in my life. Lots of things were changing in Mary Ann's life too, but it didn't seem like those things bothered her in the same way they did me.

In fact, it didn't seem like they bothered her at all.

Today

That was last night, and today when Mary Ann and I woke up, the moving truck was already next door loading up boxes.

"Would anyone like a doughnut?" Dad asked when we went into the kitchen.

Mary Ann took two. But I couldn't even eat a bite of one. When Mary Ann finished, we went next door. I stayed until the movers had loaded up the last of the boxes.

"Time to go to the new house," Frank announced when they were done.

"I'll miss you so much," I said to Mary Ann as I hugged her good-bye.

"Don't be so dramatic!" said Mary Ann. "It's not like we're not going to see each other. You can come over tomorrow and help me set up my room."

"Sure," I said like that sounded like a good plan.

But as I watched their car turn off Wish Pond Road, all I could think was that I didn't like the idea of helping Mary Ann set up her new room. I wish she was still in her old room.

And I really didn't think I was being dramatic.

I was just sad. And so was Cheeseburger. When I looked at her, I couldn't help but think that she looked just as sad as I did.

FLOWER POWER

"Now is as good of a time as any to get started."

I jump when I hear the voice behind me. When I turn around, Mrs. Black is standing there with a bucket, two spades, and some gardening gloves. She hands me a pair of gloves.

"Ready?" she asks.

I raise an eyebrow. I'm not sure what Mrs. Black thinks I'm ready to do. My best friends just drove away from Wish Pond Road. The only thing I'm ready to do is go home, lie down on my bed with my cat, and cry.

Mrs. Black must be a mind reader. "Mallory, the best cure for sadness is to stay busy! We have a lot of flowers to plant this morning." She wraps an arm around my shoulders and steers me toward her house like she's not taking no for an answer.

"Gardening is a lot like painting but with flowers. Your mother told me that you're very good with color." When we get to her yard, she motions to trays of flowers and then to her empty flower beds. "First, we need to decide where everything goes. Are you up for the job?" she asks.

I nod. Even if I wasn't, I don't think I have a choice. But the truth is that it does kind of sound like fun to paint a picture with flowers. I eye the trays of pink, purple, white, and yellow flowers waiting to be planted.

"I like to arrange the flowers on top of the dirt, and once we know where we want everything to go, then we can start planting," says Mrs. Black.

I nod like that makes sense.

Mrs. Black points to a tray of pretty yellow flowers. "These are daisies," she says. "Why don't we start with them?"

I place a row of daisies along the front of Mrs. Black's flower beds. "How does that look?" I ask when I'm done.

Mrs. Black nods like she approves. Then she points to a tray of purple flowers. "These are called coneflowers," she says.

I pick one up and smile. "Purple is my favorite color," I tell Mrs. Black.

She smiles back. "Mallory, I think we were meant to be BFFs, because that's my favorite color too."

I start laughing. I don't know why that's funny to hear, but it is. I guess I never thought about grown-ups having a favorite color. I pick up a tray of coneflowers and start placing them in a row behind the daisies.

"Wow!" says Mrs. Black when I'm done. "The purple flowers look so pretty behind the yellow ones."

I couldn't agree more. When I'm done with the coneflowers, Mrs. Black hands me a tray of white flowers called asters. I line them up behind the coneflowers, and then I add a row of pink flowers that Mrs. Black says are called dahlias.

When I finish arranging the flowers, Mrs. Black and I stand back and take a look. "That looks awesome!" I say.

"You took the words right out of my mouth," says Mrs. Black. "Now it's planting time!"

We both get down on our hands and knees and start making little holes in the dirt to plant the flowers.

Mrs. Black shows me how to dig the holes so they're not too deep and not too shallow. "It's important to place the flowers just right," says Mrs. Black. She explains about the roots of the flowers taking hold and why it's important to get the right mix of soil, water, and air.

We dig holes and plant flowers all morning.

When we finish planting, Mrs. Black and I admire our work. The flowers look so pretty. "Wow! Your garden looks great!" I say to Mrs. Black.

She smiles at me. "Our garden," she says. "I couldn't have done it without you."

"Thanks for letting me help you," I say. "It was fun."

"I'm glad you liked doing it," says Mrs. Black. "Your mother and I thought it would be a good idea." She shrugs. "We thought it would help you take your mind off the fact that your friends just moved this morning."

When she says that, my smile disappears.

I look down at my watch. My friends left exactly two hours and forty-three minutes ago. I've been so busy planting flowers, I hadn't even thought of them. Until now!

"Mallory, I'd love it if you could come by and help me water the flowers," says Mrs. Black. "Maybe we can pick a morning that works for you."

"Uh, sure," I say. Then I tell her good-bye and walk back to my house.

Now that my friends are gone and the flowers are planted, I can't imagine what I'm going to do for the rest of this day.

BONDING TIME

"Mallory, how long are you going to sit at the kitchen table and stare at the banana bowl?" asks Mom.

"What else do I have to do?" I say.

Mom laughs. "Mallory, you're being silly. It's a beautiful summer day, and there are lots of things you can do."

"Who am I going to do them with?" I mumble. I don't think I should have to remind Mom that my friends moved this morning and I don't have anyone to do anything with.

But Mom has an answer for that one too. "Why don't you and Max spend some time together?"

Now it's my turn to laugh. "Max won't want to spend time with me," I say like Mom should know that idea is ridiculous without me having to tell her.

But Mom shakes her head like I'm the one who is being ridiculous. "Max!" she yells down the hall.

I'm not sure what Mom is about to do, but something tells me it's not going to be something my brother is going to like.

When he gets to the kitchen, Mom says, "Your sister is having a hard day. It would be nice if you would spend some time with her. What do you say?" Mom gives Max a *no-is-not-an-acceptable-answer* look.

"Uh, sure," says Max. But he makes a face like someone just asked him to eat a shoe.

Mom beams. "Wonderful!" she says. "You and Mallory can enjoy some sister-brother bonding time."

Max gives me a look like the only thing we have to bond over is that we have a crazy lady for a mother.

"Why don't you two go watch TV? I'll make some sandwiches for lunch and bring them to you in the den." Mom shoos us out of the kitchen.

I tuck Cheeseburger under my arm and carry her into the den. I sit down on the couch next to Max. Even though watching TV with Max is better than watching with nobody, he's not who I want to be watching TV with. I want to be with my friends.

"So what do you want to watch?" asks Max like he's stuck with me and trying to make the best of it.

I cross my arms across my chest. "I don't care," I mutter. Max picks up the remote and clicks on to the TV guide.

"How about a movie?" he asks.

I shrug.

Max lets out a breath. "OK, what about an episode of *The Amazing Race*?"

I shrug again. "I don't care what we watch."

Max groans like he's had it. "If you don't care, then we'll watch the baseball game." Max points the remote at the TV and clicks on the sports channel.

"I don't want to watch baseball," I say crossly.

"OK," says Max. "If it makes you happy, I'll watch your dumb fashion show." He scrolls through the TV guide looking for an episode of *Fashion Fran*.

But I stop him. First of all, *Fashion Fran* isn't dumb. And second, *Fashion Fran* is what Mary Ann and I always watch together. I can't watch our favorite show with my brother!

To be viewed with BEST FRIENDS only!

"No!" I say.

Max lets out a sound like he's seriously frustrated. "I just offered to watch what you like to watch," he says.

"I want to watch it with Mary Ann," I mumble.

"I know you're upset because Bird Brain and Kangaroo Boy moved, but it's not the end of the world," says Max.

I don't think I'm acting like it's the end of

the world, but I am upset that my friends just moved this morning. Plus, I don't like it when Max calls Mary Ann and Joey Bird Brain and Kangaroo Boy. "Please don't call my friends names," I say.

Max rolls his eyes. "That's not the point," Max says. "The point is they moved, but they didn't go far. You'll still see them. No big deal. Get used to it."

I don't say anything.

"Earth to Mallory," says my brother. "Get used to it! Get used to it! Get used to it!"

I gasp. I can't believe what he just said and how he said it. "Stop it! You know saying things three times is what Mary Ann and I do!"

Max slaps his forehead like I'm being a total baby and he can't take another minute with me. "Mom might call this bonding time, but I call it stupid," says Max.

I start to tell Max he should apologize for saying that, but I don't say anything because Mom walks into the den with two plates of grilled cheese sandwiches.

"Lunch!" she says. She sets the plates down on the table in front of us. Max picks up his and eats a quarter of his sandwich in one bite.

I pick up my sandwich and take a tiny nibble.

Even one of my favorite lunches doesn't taste good to me today.

I put my plate on the table and rub Cheeseburger's back. She looks like she's going to throw up. I kind of feel the same way.

POOR KITTY

"Mom, Cheeseburger threw up!" I shout as I run into the kitchen.

Mom grabs a dish towel and follows me back to the couch. I look at Cheeseburger. "She doesn't look good," I say to Mom while she starts to clean up the mess.

Even Max looks concerned. So does Champ, who is resting his head on the couch next to Cheeseburger like he wants to try to make her feel better.

I can feel tears welling up in my eyes.

Mom looks at me. "Mallory, don't panic. It's not unusual for a cat to throw up. Let's see how Cheeseburger is this afternoon. If she isn't better in a few hours, we'll call Dr. Alvarez."

I rub Cheeseburger's back. She's never been sick before. I don't want anything to be wrong with my cat.

"Why don't you let Cheeseburger rest for a few minutes?" says Mom. "Then offer her some water."

I nod and keep rubbing Cheeseburger's back.

"I'll get her water bowl," Max offers.

He looks at me like he feels bad that he was mean earlier. I'm not even mad. I just want Cheeseburger to be OK.

Max comes back with the water bowl and sets it down next to Cheeseburger. But she doesn't move.

"Oh, no," I say softly.

Mom puts her arm around me. "Give her a little time," says Mom. "Why don't you watch a show?"

Without asking what I'd like to watch, Max picks up the remote and turns on *Fashion Fran*. He sits back down on the couch next to me like he's planning to watch it too.

I can't believe that just a few minutes ago I was fighting with him about what we were going to watch. Now it doesn't even seem important.

As much as I love Fashion Fran, it's hard to enjoy listening to her talk about matching sweater sets. All I can think about is poor Cheeseburger.

As soon as the episode is over, I offer her the water bowl again. But Cheeseburger doesn't take it this time either. I call Mom back into the den.

She tries to get Cheeseburger to drink too.

"Do you think we should call Dr. Alvarez?" I ask.

"Not yet," says Mom in a reassuring voice. "Let's give her a little more time and see how she's doing. I think she just needs to rest; then she'll drink something."

I nod, but I don't say anything.

Mom can tell I'm upset. "Why don't we all watch a movie together?" she suggests.

I'm sure it's not what Max wants to do, but he doesn't argue. He scrolls through the list of movies on the TV and picks one. I know it's one he thinks I'll like.

I smile at him like I appreciate his choice, and I do.

But as the movie starts, I can hardly think about what's happening on the screen. All I can think about is Cheeseburger.

From the moment I found her when she was a baby kitten until now, she has been one of the most important things in my life.

I love her so much, and I don't know what
I'll do if anything happens to her.

The movie only lasts ninety-two minutes,
but it's the longest ninety-two minutes of
my life. Several times during the movie, I
try to get Cheeseburger to take a drink,
but she won't.

When the movie is over, I try offering her water again, but Cheeseburger won't drink anything. "I think you should call Dr. Alvarez," I say to Mom.

"I think we need to," Mom agrees.

I sit at the kitchen table while Mom calls Dr. Alvarez. I try to take a deep breath to help me relax while Mom waits for someone to answer the phone.

Then I listen as Mom explains what's wrong with Cheeseburger.

"Yes," she says into the phone. Then she follows that up with *Uh-huh* and *I see*.

"What is it?" I mouth to Mom. But she holds up a finger like she's still listening. "Yes, we can do that," she says into the phone. When Mom hangs up, we look at each other.

"Mallory, Dr. Alvarez wants us to bring in Cheeseburger so he can take a look at her himself."

She wraps an arm around me. "I'm sure Cheeseburger will be OK. Please try not to worry."

I nod, like I'm trying.

"Let's go," says Mom. She scoops her keys up off the counter and slings her purse over her shoulder.

I pick up Cheeseburger like she's a tiny, fragile baby and carry her to Mom's van as gently as I can. When I get in, I buckle my seat belt and reposition Cheeseburger so she'll be as comfortable as possible.

Then I pretend I'm at the wish pond. I squeeze my eyes shut and make a wish. I've made lots of wishes since I've lived on Wish Pond Road, but this is the most important wish I've ever made.

I wish Cheeseburger will be OK.

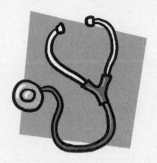

A VISIT TO
THE VET

"I'm scared," I whisper to Mom. I look around the waiting room of Dr. Alvarez's office. It looks a lot like my doctor's office, but it's filled with sick cats and dogs instead of sick kids.

I can't help but wonder what's wrong with the other animals that are here.

I feel terrible just looking at them.

At least kids can talk and tell someone what hurts. I wish Cheeseburger could tell me what's wrong with her.

Mom squeezes my hand. I know she's trying to make me feel better.

"Cheeseburger McDonald," I hear a voice say.

I look up. There's a lady in green scrubs with a clipboard at the door. She motions for Mom and me to follow her. I stand up with Cheeseburger.

We walk behind her to a room with two chairs, a small exam table, and a shelf full of what looks like pet medicines. "Can you please tell me exactly what happened?" asks the vet's assistant.

I tell her how Cheeseburger threw up and wouldn't drink anything all afternoon.

The assistant nods and makes some notes in Cheeseburger's chart. "The doctor will be here shortly," she says.

"The doctor is here!" Dr. Alvarez smiles as he walks into the room.

The assistant hands him Cheeseburger's chart, and he starts reading.

He looks at me when he's done. "Can you tell me when Cheeseburger first showed signs of distress?"

I think back to this morning when Mary Ann and Joey were leaving Wish Pond Road. Cheeseburger looked distressed then. I tell Dr. Alvarez about it.

"Do you think Cheeseburger is so sad about my friends leaving Wish Pond Road that it made her sick?"

Dr. Alvarez smiles at Mom and then looks at me kindly. "Friends moving can be sad," he says. "But I don't think that's Cheeseburger's problem. Let's take a look and see if we can figure out what's going on."

The assistant takes Cheeseburger's temperature. Then Dr. Alvarez listens to

Cheeseburger's heart and lungs. He looks inside her mouth and squeezes her tummy. It's pretty much the same thing that happens when I'm sick and go to the doctor.

Then Dr. Alvarez pulls up the fur on the top of Cheeseburger's neck. I don't have fur, but even if I did, my doctor has never done anything like that.

When Dr. Alvarez is finished doing the exam, he doesn't say a word. He rubs his chin like he's thinking.

"What's wrong with Cheeseburger?" I ask quietly. I cross my toes inside my sneakers that Dr. Alvarez is going to say it's nothing bad.

He clears his throat. "I'm not sure yet," he says. Then he explains to me that he pulled the fur on the top of Cheeseburger's neck to see if she's dehydrated.

"Cheeseburger needs fluids," he says. "I'd like to keep her overnight to make sure she's hydrated and to run some tests."

I can't believe what I just heard. "You want Cheeseburger to sleep here?" I ask.

Dr. Alvarez looks at Mom. "Dehydration in pets can be serious. We need to figure out what's going on."

Serious. I don't like that word. "It's bad, isn't it?"

Dr. Alvarez shakes his head. "I didn't say it was bad," he said. "I just want to be cautious. We will know more when we have the test results back."

Mom puts an arm around me. "Mallory, it will be fine. Cheeseburger will get the fluids she needs, and we'll know more about her condition tomorrow."

Dr. Alvarez nods like he's confirming that what Mom said is true.

But I don't see how this is going to be fine. Cheeseburger has to sleep here. "Don't you think Cheeseburger would feel better if she's with me at home?" I ask.

Dr. Alvarez gives me a sympathetic look. "I know this is hard," he says. "But we'll take good care of Cheeseburger."

He nods at his assistant, who takes

Cheeseburger off the examining table. She looks like she's getting ready to take her away. It reminds me of the scene in the  *Wizard of Oz* when the Wicked Witch of the West tries to take Toto from Dorothy.

I don't want her to take my cat.

She smiles at me sweetly, like she understands how I'm feeling. She holds Cheeseburger out to me. I take her and give her a big hug. "Don't be scared," I say to my cat.

I want to cry, but I hold back my tears. I need to be brave for Cheeseburger. I don't want her to be any more scared than she already is.

I kiss the tip of her nose. It feels drier than usual. Then I hand her to the nurse.

"We'll call you tomorrow as soon as we know something," says Dr. Alvarez.

Mom thanks Dr. Alvarez. Then she puts her arm around my shoulders, and we walk together to the van.

Mom starts the engine, but we don't even make it out of the parking lot before the tears I held back in Dr. Alvarez's office start streaming down my face.

GIRL ALONE

By Mallory McDonald
Once upon a time there was a sweet,
smart, cute little girl who had a sweet,
smart, cute little cat. The little girl loved
her cat. They were inseparable, which
means they did everything together.

If the girl was doing her homework
(which she didn't always like doing), her
cat sat with her while she did it.

If the girl was watching TV (which she always liked doing), her cat would snuggle up by her side and watch with her.

And every night when the little girl went to sleep, her cat slept on her pillow right next to her. They led a very happy life together until one terrible day when everything went wrong.

It started when the little girl's best friends, who lived next door to her, moved to another house across town. Telling them good-bye made the little girl sad.

SaD GiRL

Even though she got to plant a very pretty flower garden after they left, when she finished planting, she started to feel sad all over again.

She stayed sad, so her mother made her brother watch TV with her. It wasn't what he wanted to do, so he was mean to her.

Sadder girl

This made the little girl even sadder.

Then, when she didn't think it was possible to feel even sadder than she was already feeling, something happened that made her the saddest she'd ever been.

Her sweet, smart, cute little cat got sick and had to go to the vet. And if that wasn't bad enough, the vet said he had to run some tests and that her cat had to stay at his office!

After the little girl left her cat at the vet's office, she cried so much that when she looked

Saddest ← this girl has ever been!

at herself in the mirror, she saw that her face was blotchy, her nose was red, and her eyes were swollen.

She decided it was a good thing that she was sweet and smart because she didn't think she looked very cute right then.

That night
her family and
friends knew she
was sad so they
tried to cheer
her up.

The Sweet, smart (not cute) girl.

Her mother
made her
favorite dinner.

Her father let her stay up late.

Her brother told her if she wanted to
take a bath in the bathroom they share,
he would not bang on the door and
bother her.

Her grandmother called her to see
how she was doing.

Her best friends called too. The little
girl's mom had called their parents to
tell them what happened, and they
wanted to cheer her up.

The little girl appreciated that her family and friends were all trying to make her feel better. But she was still very worried.

Best friends ever but too far away!

So she went on the computer and looked up sick cats. She read about cats that get sick. Then she looked up seriously sick cats. Even though everyone had told her not to worry, Dr. Alvarez had used the word SERIOUS so she felt like she should look it up.

But when she read about seriously sick cats, she felt even worse than she had all day.

It made her miss her friends. It made her worry about her cat and miss her too. The little girl felt alone.

All alone.

No friends. No cat. Just her, alone, in her bed with a box of tissues.

The little girl didn't want to feel that way. She decided to draw a picture. She liked drawing pictures, so she thought it might make her feel better.

When she was done, she looked at the picture she had drawn. But this picture was different from all the other pictures she had ever drawn.

This one was the saddest picture ever.

THE END

AT THE WISH POND

When I look at my clock, it says 7:22 a.m. I roll over and put my hand on the spot where Cheeseburger always sleeps.

I hoped I would be able to sleep late. All I want is for this day to pass quickly and for Dr. Alvarez to call.

I roll over and close my eyes and try to go back to sleep. But I can't sleep. My brain is too busy thinking about Cheeseburger.

When I look at the clock again, it's only 7:24. I don't know how I'm going to be able to wait until Dr. Alvarez calls.

I sit up in bed and listen for a minute.

But my house is totally quiet. I get out of bed, slip on some leggings, a T-shirt, and my sneakers. I pull my hair up into a ponytail. Then I walk down the hall toward the front door.

There's someplace I need to go.

Usually when I go to this place, I take Cheeseburger with me. But since she's not here, I walk to the wish pond by myself.

When I get there, I sit on the edge of the pond.

I run my fingers through the rocks at the edge of the wish pond. When I first moved to Wish Pond Road, Joey told me about wish pebbles.

He said that they're shiny pebbles and that when you find one, you throw it in the wish pond and make your wish. He told me when you make a wish with a wish pebble, your wish is supposed to come true.

I look until I find the shiniest pebble I can find. I curl my fingers around it tightly, squeeze my eyes shut, and throw it into the wish pond.

I wish that Cheeseburger will be OK.

When I'm done wishing, I keep my eyes shut for a long time. This wish has to come true. I don't know what I'd do without Cheeseburger.

My eyes are still closed when I feel someone tap me on my shoulder. Before I even open my eyes, I know who it is.

"May I join you?" asks Dad.

He smiles and offers me his hand. I take it, and we sit down together on the bench beside the wish pond. We've had lots of talks at the wish pond, and I can tell we're about to have another one. "Sweet Potato, I know this is hard."

I nod.

He wraps an arm around me. "Sometimes things happen that you don't want to happen. Change is a big part of life. You need to try to be open to changes. It's not always easy." Dad smiles at me in a dad-like way. "Part of growing up is learning how to handle whatever comes your way and making the best of it."

"I know," I say to Dad. "It's just hard to make the best of Cheeseburger being sick."

Dad nods like he totally gets it. "It's a shame when things happen that we don't want to happen. But it doesn't mean that you should expect the worst." Dad looks at me like he wants to make sure I hear what he says next. "Dr. Alvarez will call us today and tell us how Cheeseburger is doing. Hopefully, she will be just fine."

I know Dad is trying to make me feel

better, but I feel like someone just punched me in the stomach.

"What if Cheeseburger isn't fine?" I don't even want to say the other thing I'm thinking, but the words come out before I can stop them. "What if she doesn't make it?"

When I woke up this morning, I didn't think I'd be having a serious talk like this, but now that it has started, I want to know what Dad thinks.

He looks at me for a long time before he answers. "Mallory, I think Cheeseburger *will* be fine. But unfortunately, most things don't last forever. It's important to appreciate what you have while you have it."

Dad looks at me to see if I get what he's talking about. I don't like thinking about it, but I get it.

Dad continues. "You should always make the most of the time you have with important people—and pets—in your life. That way, even if there comes a time that they're not with you anymore, you will always have the good memories of the times you shared together."

Dad looks at me like what he's about to say next is important. "Memories are forever."

I nod to show him I get that too. And in one way, I like it.

It doesn't make me feel better about the fact that Cheeseburger is sick, but it is nice to know that I'll always have the good memories of all the times I've shared with Cheeseburger and my friends.

"Thanks, Dad," I say. I stand up like we're done talking, but Dad doesn't move. He pats the bench like he wants me to sit back down because he has something else he wants to say.

When I sit, Dad starts talking again. "Mallory, we've talked a lot about Cheeseburger. I know how upset you are about Mary Ann and Joey moving too."

I look up at Dad. I'm not sure what he's going to say next that I haven't already heard.

"I know how much you like spending time with your friends," says Dad. "You'll still see them a lot, but you don't have to be with them all the time."

Dad pauses. "I guess what I'm trying to say is that it can also be nice to have some time on your own. Maybe you should use it as an opportunity."

Now I'm confused. "To do what?" I ask.

"To do something that you like doing. You like coming to the wish pond alone. It's when you do some of your best thinking."

Dad's right. I do like to come alone to the wish pond when I want to think.

"I'll bet there are other things you like to do that you wouldn't do with Mary Ann or Joey or Chloe Jennifer."

"You mean like when I played on the basketball team even though Mary Ann and Chloe Jennifer didn't want to?"

Dad nods like he likes that example. Then he gives me one of his own.

"When I was your age, I loved building model airplanes. I still had fun with my friends, but I liked building model airplanes on my own," says Dad.

"I don't think I'd have fun building model airplanes," I tell him.

Dad laughs. "Probably not. Everybody's different. I'm just saying that you might want to try exploring some of your own interests."

"I'll think about it," I say to Dad.

He smiles like he's glad to hear that.

"We better go back," I say. "I want to be home when Dr. Alvarez calls."

Dad and I stand up. He gives me a big hug, and then we walk home.

A NEW DAY

"I'll get it!" I say when the phone rings.
That's what I've said every time it's
rung this morning. Now it's 11:25, and I
still haven't gotten the call I've been
waiting for.

"Do you think we should call Dr.
Alvarez's office?" I ask Mom for what I'm
sure must be the three thousandth time.

But Mom has the same answer she's
had all morning, which is that Dr. Alvarez

promised to call as soon as he knows something.

I look at my watch and blow a piece of hair off my face. Then I stare at the phone.

Ring. Phone. Ring.

I say those words over and over again in my head, like they're a magic spell that will make the phone ring.

It works! The phone rings, and it's the call I've been waiting for.

I listen carefully as the voice on the other end tells me that it's Dr. Alvarez's office calling and that Cheeseburger is ready to be picked up.

"Is she OK?" I ask.

The voice tells me that Dr. Alvarez would like to see Mom and me but that Cheeseburger is fine. I give Mom the thumbs-up sign. She looks as relieved as I feel.

"We'll be right there!" I say.

Mom doesn't ask any questions. She just grabs her keys off the counter, and we both head for the van.

When we get to Dr. Alvarez's office, the waiting room is filled to capacity with people and their pets. I suck in my breath. I don't know how I'm going to be able to wait even another minute to see Cheeseburger. But I don't have to.

The assistant who helped us yesterday is at the front desk. "I know you're anxious to see Cheeseburger," she says. Then she motions for Mom and me to follow her.

"Wait here," she says when we get to the same waiting room we were in yesterday.

She leaves and when she comes back, she's carrying Cheeseburger.

"Cheeseburger!" I say.

The assistant hands her to me, and I can tell my cat is just as happy to see me as I am to see her. I cradle her in my arms. When she nuzzles her nose into me, I start smiling and can't stop.

"Mallory!" Dr. Alvarez smiles as he walks into the room. "You look much happier today than you did yesterday."

I nod. "I am happy."

"I'm happy too," says Dr. Alvarez. "Cheeseburger is going to be fine. She was dehydrated, and we gave her fluids. However, the tests we ran were inconclusive."

I give Dr. Alvarez a *could-you-please-talk-so-I-can-understand-what-you're-saying* look.

He smiles like that's a look he's seen before.

He starts again. "We're not sure what was wrong with Cheeseburger. It was probably just a virus—nothing serious. All her organs are functioning normally." Dr. Alvarez pauses and looks at me like he's about to give me some important information and I need to listen carefully.

"Mallory, for the next week, you'll need to give Cheeseburger lots of TLC. It's normal for sick cats to lose their appetite. Encourage Cheeseburger to eat. You might even have to feed her by hand for a day or two. If you see that she doesn't fall back into her normal routine, you need to call me."

"I can do that," I tell Dr. Alvarez.

"Good," he says like he's glad to know his patient will be in good hands. "Then you may take Cheeseburger home now."

As Mom and I walk to the van with Cheeseburger, I can't believe how much happier I am leaving than I was when I walked in.

When Mom and I get home, Max and Dad are waiting for us. I tell them both what Dr. Alvarez said. Everyone looks happy, especially Champ. I think he missed Cheeseburger as much as I did.

"This calls for a celebration!" says Dad. "Why don't we go out for pizza?"

I shake my head. "I'm not going anywhere!" I tell Dad what Dr. Alvarez said about watching Cheeseburger. "I'm not leaving my cat's side for a whole week," I say.

Dad smiles. "Well, if you won't go out for pizza, we can bring it in."

I tell Dad that that's a great idea. I was so worried about Cheeseburger today that I hardly ate a bite. "I'm starving!" I say. Dad laughs. When he leaves to get the pizza, I carry Cheeseburger into the kitchen. I put a little bit of her food into a small bowl. I sit down with her in my lap and feed her one piece at a time. When she's done eating, she purrs like she's happy.

I pick her up and carry her to the couch. I put her down beside me. She closes her eyes, and I rub her back while she sleeps.

When the doorbell rings, Cheeseburger's eyes fly open. "Mallory, that must be Dad with the pizza," says Mom. "Can you please open the door for him?"

"Sure," I say and spring off the couch. I can't wait for the pizza! But when I open the door, there's a whole lot more there than Dad and pizza. Mary Ann and Joey are there too!

"Surprise!" they say together.

I stand there with my mouth open. I can't believe they're here.

"Your mom called Colleen and told her how your visit to the vet went," Joey explains. "Colleen was going to bring us over to see you."

Mary Ann picks up where Joey leaves off. "But your mom said she would text your dad, who went to get pizza, and he would come pick us up." She grins. "We thought Cheeseburger should have a homecoming party, so here we are!" Now it's my turn to grin. It's nice to know that even though my best friends don't live next door anymore, they're still here when I need them.

Dad looks at all of us and smiles. "Pizza time!" he says. We follow Dad into the kitchen.

"Mmm!" I say as I bite into a slice of pepperoni pizza.

"Double mmm!" says Mary Ann when she takes a bite.

"Triple mmm!" says Joey when it's his turn.

Max rolls his eyes at us like we're all annoying and babyish. But I can tell he's in a good mood too. My family and friends are as happy as I am that Cheeseburger is OK.

When Joey's dad comes to pick up Mary Ann and Joey, Mary Ann hugs me good-bye. "You have to come over tomorrow and help me set up my room!"

I hesitate. I'm not sure Mary Ann is going to like what I say next. I tell her what Dr. Alvarez said. "I'm not going anywhere for a week," I tell her.

Mary Ann groans like that's terrible news.

But to me, it's not so terrible. I wish Mary Ann still lived next door and didn't have a new room that needed setting up. I wish she could just hang out with me while I cat-sit. I really wish Cheeseburger hadn't gotten sick in the first place. But I'm so happy that Cheeseburger is OK that it's hard to be upset about anything.

"One week, but that's it!" says Mary Ann.

I nod my head. "One week and I'll be there," I promise. "I'm already counting the days!"

SURPRISES

"Get off the phone already!" says Max.

I wave at my brother like he should stop talking. Then I cover my ear that's not next to the receiver so I can hear what Mary Ann is saying.

"See you soon," I say as I hang up.

Max looks at me and shakes his head. "Do you know how many times a day you talk to her?"

I start counting in my head. But it's a lot,

so I give up. "Sorry," I say to Max. I know I've been a phone hog lately, but I haven't left the house for a week.

I've been by Cheeseburger's side the whole time.

Actually, she's been by my side the whole time. She kept me company while I watched *Fashion Fran*, read the gardening book Mrs. Black dropped off for me, and wrote letters to Chloe Jennifer.

She kept me company while I did other things too—things I hadn't planned to do.

Max rolls his eyes at me as I leave the kitchen, but I don't mind. I'm too happy right now to let anything bother me.

Mom and I took Cheeseburger back to Dr. Alvarez this morning for a check up, and he said she's fine. So this afternoon, I'm going to Mary Ann and Joey's house.

For the first time!

"Mallory!" Mary Ann screams as soon as I get out of the car in front of the Winstons' new house. She and Joey are waiting for me on their front porch. Mary Ann flies down the sidewalk to meet me. She gives me a big hug. "I'm so happy you're here!" she says.

"Me too!" I say.

"There's a reason she's happy you're here," says Joey as he comes up to greet me. "Her room is a mess, and she's been waiting for you to get here and help her set it up!"

Mary Ann makes a guilty face. "That's true!" she says like she's not ashamed to admit it. Then she pokes Joey in the ribs. "Your room isn't any better."

Joey laughs. "Unfortunately, that's also true."

I loop my arms through both of theirs. "Don't worry," I say. "I'll help both of you."

They both smile like they're glad to hear that.

"So this is our house," says Joey as we walk in the front door. I take a look around at the wood floors and light yellow walls. All the furniture that was in the Winstons' old house is in this one. "Nice!" I say.

Joey and Mary Ann show me the living room, the dining room, the den, and then the kitchen.

"Mallory!" says Colleen when we walk into the kitchen. "It's so good to see you!" She's feeding baby Charlie. He actually looks like he's grown since I saw him a week ago.

Frank and Grandpa Winston come in the kitchen when they hear all the noise. "Look who's here," says Frank. He high-fives me.

"Are you hungry?" asks Grandpa Winston.

Mary Ann and Joey look at each other and shake their heads. "Sorry, Grandpa," says Joey. "Mallory is here to help us set up our rooms. She doesn't have time to eat."

Grandpa Winston laughs. "I've seen both of your rooms." He winks at me. "I'm sure you're going to work up quite an appetite this afternoon!"

"Oh no!" I say to Joey and Mary Ann.

"Are you ready?" Joey asks.

"I think so!" I say as I follow my friends up the stairs.

We pass a room with a *Baby Sleeps Here* sign on the door. Then we pass another door with a sign that says *Keep Out*. "I know who sleeps *there*," I say to Joey and Mary Ann. They both laugh.

Winnie had that sign on her door at their old house. I guess some things never change.

The next room we come to is Joey's. He cracks open the door slowly. There are boxes and stuff everywhere. It's a huge mess. I'm not even sure where to start.

"Maybe you want to help Mary Ann first," says Joey.

"Uh, sure." I can't think of anything else to say.

Joey laughs. "But you have to promise to come back."

"No problem," I tell him. Then I follow Mary Ann. She leads me down the hall and pushes open a door with a giant sunflower on it. Her new room looks almost exactly like her old room. It's painted the same color, and she has the same furniture. She even has the same posters on the wall.

"Wow!" I say, smiling. "I feel like we're still in your old room."

"The only difference is that my stuff is all over the place," says Mary Ann, pointing to the boxes on the floor.

"And it's on the second floor, which

means it would be hard for me to climb in your window," I say.

Mary Ann laughs at that.

"Ready to work?" she asks.

I nod and we dig in. We work all afternoon until everything is put away.

"Wow!" says Mary Ann when we're done. "I can't believe how good it looks. Thanks so much for helping me."

"Sure," I say as I look around her room. "Every single thing is in perfect order."

Mary Ann nods. "It will probably never be this neat again."

We both know that's the truth and crack up.

"OK," says Mary Ann. "I have a surprise for you." She makes me sit on her chair. "Close your eyes," she says.

When she tells me to open them, I can't believe what I'm seeing. Actually, I'm not really sure what I'm seeing. Mary Ann is holding something that looks like a cake on a platter, but it doesn't look like the kind of cake you would want to eat.

"What is it?" I ask.

Mary Ann smiles. "It's a Friendship

Cake." She holds it closer so I can get a better view.

I take a good, long look. There's a lot to see!

Mary Ann used a round box shaped like a cake and glued pictures of us all over the box. There are all sorts of pictures of all the fun things we've done together over the years.

There are pictures of us from camp and at home and on Halloween and when we went on the cruise. There's a picture of us with Fashion Fran when we went to New York and got to be on her show. There are even pictures of us when we were little. Plus, Mary Ann added cute stickers of things I love like hearts and cats and smiley faces and fashion. She put the cake on a cake stand so it really looks like a cake.

"I love it!" I say to Mary Ann.

She grins. "I wanted to do something nice to show you how much our friendship means to me. But I didn't want to make another scrapbook." She paused. "I wanted to do something new and different."

She looks at me and continues talking. "Mal, I know you've had a hard time with the move. I guess with the move, a lot of things are different. I guess what I'm saying is that when things change, you just have to deal with it. Do you know what I mean?"

I do know what she means. It's kind of the same thing Dad talked to me about at the wish pond. But the truth is that while it might be easy for Mary Ann to do, it's not always so easy for me. I look down at a scab on my knee.

"I have had a hard time," I say. "I've been really sad that we don't live next door to each other anymore."

I pause. What I have to say next might not be something she wants to hear, but I feel like I need to say it. "I guess it kind of bothered me that it didn't seem like it was hard for you."

Mary Ann shakes her head. "It's not that it wasn't hard. Maybe I just don't show it the same way you do." She shrugs. "Even though we're best friends, we handle things differently."

I nod. I see where she's coming from.

Mary Ann gives me an *enough-of-the-serious-talk* look. "We might have some differences, but there are some things we both like to do, like watch Fashion Fran. Now that Cheeseburger is better, you can come over every day and we can hang out just like we always have."

"Not every day," I say.

Mary Ann looks at me like she's not sure what I'm talking about.

"I'm helping Mrs. Black in her garden on Mondays," I say.

Mary Ann makes a face like I said I wanted to jump off a bridge or eat a raw onion. "Ugh! That'll be so boring."

"It's actually kind of fun," I say. "But I'll be doing something else that's even more fun."

"What is it?" asks Mary Ann. I take a

deep breath and start explaining. "While Cheeseburger was sick, I spent a lot of time just sitting next to her, rubbing her back, and looking at her. One day, I picked up my sketchpad and started drawing her. And once I started drawing, I couldn't stop. I drew her from every angle in lots of different ways."

I pause and look at Mary Ann. She looks like she's waiting for me to continue. So I do.

"I really enjoyed drawing her, so I asked Mom if I could take an art class. She signed me up for one on Tuesdays and Thursdays at the Fern Falls Youth Center."

Mary Ann frowns a little. "Taking an art class doesn't sound like a fun thing to do in the summer," she says.

"It does to me," I say. Then I shrug. "I guess that's just another way we're different."

Mary Ann nods like she gets what I'm saying. Then she smiles at me. "Well, there's one thing that will always be the same."

I smile back. I think I know what she's going to say.

"No matter where we live, we'll always be best friends," says Mary Ann.

I couldn't have said it better myself. I hold up my pinky. Mary Ann hooks hers around mine, and we pinky swear.

Some things might change. But some things are forever.

THE MEANING
OF FOREVER

"Mallory, dinner!"

I hear Mom's voice from the kitchen. I put my drawing pad down on my bed, and then I take another look at the friendship cake Mary Ann gave me this afternoon. It looks so cute on my dresser. I really love seeing the pictures of all the fun times Mary Ann and I have had together.

I skip from my room toward the kitchen. Something smells delicious. But when I get to the end of the hallway, Mom stops me. She holds up a hand, stop-sign style.

"I have a surprise for you!" Mom covers my eyes and walks me into the kitchen.

I sniff the air. I think I know what the surprise is. "Are we having spaghetti and meatballs?" I ask Mom. She knows that's my favorite dinner.

"Would you like to see?" asks Mom. I can hear the smile in her voice. When she takes her hands away from my face, I see spaghetti and meatballs, but I see something else too.

"Grandma!" I sprint across the kitchen.

"Honey Bee!" Grandma gives me a huge hug.

"I'm so glad you're here," I say as my family sits down at the table. Max helps

himself to the spaghetti and then passes
it to me. I pile noodles and sauce on my
plate, top it with a big meatball, and take
a bite.

"So how's my girl?" asks Grandma.

Mom, Dad, and Max all look at me.

"My summer got off to a rough start," I
tell Grandma. "But some good things have
happened too."

She fills her plate with spaghetti and meatballs. "Want to tell me about it?"

I put my fork down and tell Grandma about my friends leaving Wish Pond Road. Then I tell her about Cheeseburger getting sick and how I had to watch her and take care of her.

"I was really upset, especially when Cheeseburger got sick. But I feel better now that I know she's OK," I say. "Even though Mary Ann and Joey don't live next door anymore, I know we'll still see each other a lot. Chloe Jennifer and I are pen pals. It has been fun writing to her and getting letters. *And* I'm helping Mrs. Black in her garden. *And* I'm taking an art class."

Grandma smiles. "That's a lot of *ands*, but they're all good ones."

I nod.

"I know how hard and scary it can be when things change," says Grandma. "And especially when a lot of changes happen at the same time. It sounds like you're learning to handle those changes. I'm proud of you."

"Thanks, Grandma!" I say.

One of my favorite things about my grandma is that she always gets it.

Grandma smiles at me, and then she clears her throat like she has something important to say.

Mom gives Max a *put-your-fork-down-and-listen* look. He doesn't seem too happy about it, but he does it.

"Change is part of life," she says. "But I have a strategy for dealing with it. I'm pretty old, and it has worked well for me for a very long time."

I know Grandma, and I know she wants

me to ask her what her strategy is, so I do.

"Well," says Grandma. "My strategy for dealing with change—and life in general—is to take things one day at a time. Some days are good, and some days aren't. But it's all manageable if you just take it one day at a time."

Max gives Grandma a smile like he actually does appreciate her advice. Then he goes back to eating his spaghetti.

"That sounds like a good idea to me," I say. It's what I did when Cheeseburger came home from the vet's office, and it worked.

Just hearing what Grandma has to say makes me feel better, and it makes me hungrier than I have been for a long time. I take another meatball and take a big bite.

"Mmm," I say between bites of spaghetti. "This is really good!"

I don't know why what I said is funny, but Mom and Dad look at each other and laugh.

I wipe my mouth with my napkin. "What's so funny?" I ask.

Dad clears his throat. "We've heard a lot this summer about all the things that have changed in your life, but some things have stayed the same." I look at Dad. There's a twinkle in his eye so I know he's teasing me.

But still, I can't imagine what he's going to say. "Like what?" I ask.

He points his fork toward the second meatball on top of my spaghetti. "You still like spaghetti and meatballs."

"A lot!" says Mom.

"And you still hog the phone," says Max.

"Hey!" I say to Max like he'd better watch what he's saying about me.

"Sorry," said Max. "I was wrong about that."

I can't believe my brother is going to apologize to me! Some things really do change and for the better! But Max isn't finished.

"Something *is* different," he says. "Now that Bird Brain doesn't live next door anymore, you're a bigger phone hog than ever!"

"Max!" my parents say at the same time. But I know they're not really mad at him, and I'm not either. How can I be mad? I have a lot of things to be happy about.

I have a great family and friends. Grandma is here. Cheeseburger is healthy. I'm taking an art class that I'm really excited about. In a few weeks, Mom, Dad, Max, and I are going to the Grand Canyon. And in the fall, I'm going to fifth grade!

I know there will be lots more changes when school starts. I have a feeling it won't always be easy, but I'm going to try my best to handle whatever comes my way.

And I'm going to do it one day at a time.

FRIENDSHIP CAKE

Here's Mary Ann's recipe for Friendship Cake. I love the one that Mary Ann made for me. I know if you make your own Friendship Cake for a special friend, your friend will love it too!

Have fun baking!

Recipe for Friendship Cake

Supplies:

memories of fun and laughter with your
    friend
photo paper
old photos of fun times with your friend
scissors
1 round box from a craft store
cute stickers for decorating such as
    flowers, hearts, and butterflies
fast-drying glue

Directions:

    1. Make copies of all the photos on
photo paper.
    2. Cut out the top half of some
photos that will wrap around the lid of

the box, so you can see the silhouettes of your friends or at least their head shapes.

    3. Add another row of photos below the first row and repeat again below that row until the box is covered.

    4. Glue additional photos to cover the top of the box, so you can enjoy them when looking down at the cake.

    5. Add stickers to fill in gaps between photos and to add splashes of color.

    6. Set cake on a cake plate to display.

    7. Present cake to your friend.

    8. Enjoy remembering all the fun times you've spent together!

A LETTER

Dear Chloe Jennifer,

Thanks for the Get Well card you sent to Cheeseburger! I put it up on the bulletin board in my room. It made her feel better when she was sick, and it made me feel good too!

And thanks for being such a good friend from so far away! Even though it's a whole lot more fun when you're actually here, it has been fun being pen pals!

I have been super busy since the last time I wrote you. I've been helping Mrs. Black in her garden. It's fun to take care of the flowers and watch them grow. It's even fun to spend time with Mrs. Black.

I'm also taking the art class I told you about in my last letter, and I LOVE it! My teacher is named Serena. She's a grown-up, but we don't have to call her mrs. (or ms. or miss). She lets us call her by her first name because she says we're all artists, which makes us all equals! How cool is that!?!

She has posters up all over the art room that say things like: *Color your world happy* and *Live life in color.* Here's a drawing of one of my favorite posters.

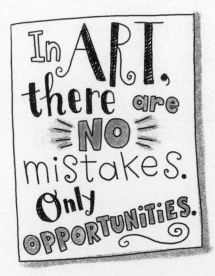

I've already learned a ton about art, like drawing techniques and how to use watercolors, oil paints, and chalk.

But the coolest thing I've learned has been outside the classroom. I've learned that it can be fun doing things on your own, especially things that you really like doing.

Like art!

At the start of the summer, I didn't see anything good about you or Mary Ann or Joey not being on Wish Pond Road.

I hope this doesn't make you feel bad to hear this (and trust me, I can't wait until you come home!), but if you all hadn't been gone and Cheeseburger hadn't gotten sick and I hadn't spent time at home drawing her, I never would have decided I wanted to take an art class. And now I'm really glad I've done that!

The other thing I learned is that when you don't have something, it makes you appreciate it more. I know that sounds a little weird, but whenever I go to Mary Ann and Joey's house, I'm extra excited to see them, and when I get a letter from you, I feel the same way.

OK. Enough about all the stuff I've learned.

I've made lots of drawings and paintings, and I made a couple for you.

Here's a picture I drew of you. Since you're in Atlanta, I had to draw it from a photo, but I think it looks pretty much like you.

I hope you think so too!

Here's a
picture I drew
of Freckles.
Since he's in
Atlanta with
you, I had to
draw him from
a photo too!

And last but
not least, here's
a drawing of my
mailbox. Since we're
pen pals, I've been
going there a lot
this summer!

I hope you like my drawings. It's fun being pen pals this summer, but one thing is for sure: I can't wait for you to get back. Wish Pond Road isn't the same without you. I can't believe that when you come back, we'll be starting fifth grade!

That's it for now. Oops—sorry, one more thing . . . write back soon!

Big, huge hugs and kisses!
Mallory

Darby Creek
A division of Lerner Publishing Group, Inc.
241 First Avenue North
Minneapolis, MN 55401 USA

For reading levels and more information, look up this title at
www.lernerbooks.com.

Cover background © Hlib Marderosiants/Shutterstock.com.

Main body text set in LumarcLL 14/20. Typeface provided by Linotype.

Library of Congress Cataloging-in-Publication Data

Friedman, Laurie B., 1964–
        Change Is in the Air, Mallory / by Laurie Friedman ; illustrated by
Jennifer Kalis.
            pages   cm. — (Mallory ; #24)
        Summary: Ten-year-old Mallory is not looking forward to the summer as
her friends are either moving or away on vacation, but she soon learns that
some changes can be good, and some things are forever.
        ISBN 978-1-4677-0924-8 (trade hard cover : alk. paper)
        ISBN 978-1-4677-8822-9 (EB pdf)
        [1. Change—Fiction. 2. Friendship—Fiction.] I. Kalis, Jennifer, illustrator.
II. Title.
PZ7.F89773Fo 2015
[Fic]—dc23   2014025034

Manufactured in the United States of America
1 — BP — 7/15/15

SUSTAINABLE FORESTRY INITIATIVE

Certified Chain of Custody
Promoting Sustainable Forestry
www.sfiprogram.org
SFI-01268

SFI label applies to the text stock